BEAUTIFUL TOXICITY

YOU DON'T HAVE TO STAY WHERE YOU ARE.
HEALING IS JUST A FRIENDSHIP AWAY.

WRITTEN BY: ONTARIA KIM WILSON

PUBLISHED BY: Pen Legacy® (penlegacy.com)
TYPESETTING & LAYOUT BY: Junnita Jackson (www.theliarscraft.com)

DISCLAIMER

Although you may find the teachings, life lessons and examples in this book to be useful, the book is sold with the understanding that neither the author nor Pen Legacy, LLC. are engaged in presenting any legal, relationship, financial, emotional, or health advice.

Any person who's experiencing financial, anxiety, depression, health, or relationship issues should consult with a licensed therapist, advisor, licensed psychologist, or any qualified professional before commencing into anything described in this book. This book's intent is to provide you with the writer's account and experience with overcoming life matters. All results will differ; however, our goal is to provide you with our "take" on how to overcome and be resilient when faced with circumstances. There are lessons in every blessing.

Library of Congress Cataloging – in- Publication Data has been applied for.

ISBN: 978-0-9600483-8-0

PRINTED IN THE UNITED STATES OF AMERICA.

CONTENTS

Beautiful Toxicity
The Stage Play

WRITTEN & DIRECTED BY
ONTARIA KIM WILSON

JULY 28TH

"THROUGH TRANSPARENCY, TRUST & LOVE THEY REALIZE THAT THEIR
SISTERHOOD IS THE CONDUIT FOR THEIR HEALING"

Beautiful Toxicity

THE SCREEN PLAY

TICKETS ON SALE ON EVENTBRITE.COM!

ARTS BANK
601 S. BROAD STREET
PHILADELPHIA, PA 19147
7:00PM

A MULTI-CULTURAL FILM

"A LIVE STAGE PRODUCTION"

Free Smith is a freelance writer and poet from Cherry Hill New Jersey. On a trip to visit her husband Les (an entertainment consultant) in the Middle East in the small but vast island of Abu Khali she gets more than what she bargains for.

For months she has anticipated being in the arms of her husband whom she's been apart from for a few months. Their relationship has grown astoundingly stronger during their separation. The cliché, "absence makes the heart grow fonder", rings volumes regarding these two love birds. No, it's not easy being away from your loved one but thank God for cells phones, whatsapp, face book, and all the other digital outlets available to make it possible for a face to face talk every day. But when she sees him in the physical for the first time, she's introduced to a shocking new way of life dictated by Islamic law.

Upon her arrival she gets a sweet taste of the life Les has been living for the past few months. Abu Khali is nothing short of beautiful. The hospitality of the natives are bar none. The culture is breathtaking and the spirit of Abu Khali is nothing like what western media portrays through its propaganda and terroristic war stricken imagery. Quickly Free begins to feel at home and free from the stresses of big city living that she's known most of her life.

During her stay in Abu Khali Les introduces her to a plethora of people ranging from ambassadors, fortune 500 business owners, promoters, military officers, musicians, performers. But there are a few people that will forever change her life as she knows it.

Tao, Jazmina, Nafisa, Treese, and Ngoyo are five women from different walks of life and parts of the world who have won Free's heart in the short time that she's been in Abu Khali. But it's through them that she will get the opportunity to witness the underworld of Abu Khali, hear and experience the toxicity that has shaped the lives of these beautiful women she now calls sister. While they are trapped...Free is just a visitor. Others quietly yearn to touch the shores of the United States of America. On the outside beauty rings loud but deep within toxicity enslaves them. Will freedom ever prevail in their lives or is their sisterhood enough?

PRELUDE

It's interesting the path we all travel in this thing called life. We are born into this world innocent and without agenda, we just exist having no control over what we are born into. Over time we adapt to our environment, people, sounds, smells, taste, and our own personal identity. Our family members are the first to experience our growing personalities. They are taken aback by our wittiness, spontaneity, creativity, and carefree attitudes but they always laugh and naturally just accept us as we are... without condemnation.

But, something happens in our maturation process where we abort our uniqueness and replace it with societal norms that box us in and strips us from experiencing the freedom we experienced before toxicity introduced itself. There's a passage in the bible that states "You are fearfully and wonderfully made." Now, I'm not sure why this isn't taught and instilled in every child from birth. Can you imagine the power, confidence, and conscious will to thrive we'd have if someone told us that we're perfect just the way we were and worthy of honor at all times? There would be less worry about how others perceive us and we would be less inclined to alter our dreams, passions, and authenticity to comply with what others think we should be.

In the midst of fighting to stay true to ourselves and pleasing others we acquire certain people in our lives who walk with us, talk with us, laugh with us, cry with us, debate with us, advise us, pray with us, challenge us, travel with us, encourage us, grow old with us, and stay true to us. These people are our friends. Our Best friends. Our BFF's. Our Girls. Our Tribe. What would we do without them? I would venture to say that life would be a difficult road to travel if not for the privilege of true friendship. I believe that relationships are God's way of allowing us to experience his heart and his attributes making the idea of a relationship with the creator and creation real in the hearts, minds, and souls of humanity.

Beautiful Toxicity is based on the off Broadway play written, directed, and produced by Ontaria Kim Wilson in July 2018. The story is based around Free Smith, a freelance writer from the United States, who traveled to Abu Khali (The Pink Diamond of the Middle East) to visit her husband Les who is an entertainment contractor and club manager. While there she meets a group of women from different walks of life and their relationships turn into divine connections filled with moments of unmasking deeply rooted wounds that have tormented them for years. They expose their beauty and toxicity at the same time, but through transparency, trust, and love they realize that their sisterhood is the conduit for their healing.

The hope is that everyone who walks away from this read will realize their fullest potential, release themselves from their past, and realize that true healing and freedom are more easily ascertained when you have a solid support system. You may live in your own skin, but you are not an island left to stand alone. Allow yourself to flush out the toxicity so your true beauty can live. Enjoy.

DEDICATION

I dedicate this book to those beautiful souls who have gone before us but their legacies have changed the lives of those who were fortunate to be in their presence.

Dominique (Ki Ki) Ogelsby

Sylvia Wilson

Hattie Wilder

Paul Wilder

Ronald Matthew Gregory

Tommy Wilson

Florence Smith

Thomas Clay

THE PINK DIAMOND

Google's definition of a diamond: (noun) 1. A precious stone consisting of a clear and colorless crystalline form of pure carbon, the hardest naturally occurring substance; 2. A figure with four straight sides of equal length forming two opposite acute angles and two opposite obtuse angles.

No one ever really talks about Abu Khali. It is the pink diamond of the Middle East. Tucked away between two of the most powerful countries in the region it is saturated with gold, oil, spices, international trade, culture, and some of the best entertainment the world has to offer. The streets are lined with pictures of the king and his sons. The Islamic call to prayer permeates the country throughout the day reminding everyone that respect, honor, and communication must be paid to the creator. With a mix of western culture and traditional Arab dress you find malls filled with fashion conscious shoppers adorned and splurging on high end western fashion. Then there are the souks. These street markets are full of vendors who are eager to sell and prepared to go against the slickest of bidders who come there knowing that deals are made every second of the day.

It's not strange that you're able to get a tailor made suit made out of the best fabric the Middle East has to offer for only one hundred and fifty U.S. dollars. Amazing right? I know. The beauty and richness of Abu Khali is fascinating at best. But when you step off the plane the airport immediately lets you know that you have arrived in the heart of the Middle East. The floors and chairs are shrouded with Muslim garb, prayer rooms are placed strategically in each terminal, Arabic music melodiously flows from the audio system, security is stern and hospitable as you enter customs, and the money exchange clerk politely advising that your dollar is 2.68 percent less than the dinar after you've given her a hundred dollar bill and she in turn hands you 34 dinar and 900 fils. Yup. That's like saying 34 dollars and 900 cents. Mind blowing yet enchanting. Hey! Welcome to Abu Khali.

So let me tell you...the excitement I felt when the plane landed and I was finally able to use What's-app to call my baby was indescribable. The sound of his voice and knowing that in just a matter of minutes I would be able to see him in the flesh was worth the plane's inability to land at the second layover destination because of the fog; the fear and frustration that arose when the pilot announced that we were not allowed to land and that we were running out of fuel; and my drive through and three day stay in Kuwait because no other country could accommodate our flight disembarking at their facility was oh so worth my 13,000 mile trip and the feel of his strong arms wrapped around me. Mmmm mmmm mmmm.

I'm sorry. I'm getting all juicy and running my mouth and I haven't introduced myself. My name is Free. I'm a poet and writer from the United States. I've always loved writing since I was a child and it turned out to be the very thing that I would choose as my career of choice. I'm a freelance writer who writes for film and TV. I'm traveling to Abu Khali to visit my husband who's an entertainment consultant contracted to bring live entertainment to the region. Never in a million years did I imagine having someone in my life that would know me almost as well as I know myself. The male side of me that keeps me focused, encourages me when I need it the most, but able to challenge me when I fall prey to my own doubts, frustrations, and fears. We are perfectly imperfect. Yeah...when you realize that about yourself it's easier to realize that same trait in every other person on this planet. Is it really love you ask? Ummmm...yeah. I'd travel another 13,000 miles every day for the rest of my life for this love because God gave me the best example of love through Les; and he shows it every day with grace, mercy, long suffering, relationship, ever presence, and more. Ok...I might be getting too deep for some of you, but I can't help myself. So, back to the story.

After I get my luggage, I walk through the airport toward ground transportation. Across the gate I see Pizza Hut, KFC, Taco Bell, and a tall, dark, and handsome guy with a black and white sweat suit, black baseball cap, black and white Nikes, and a beautiful smile. My heart races cause in thirty seconds I get to kiss my love and have him hold me in his arms. I cross the threshold and we are both grinning from ear to ear. Everything is familiar now. We reach each other and I release my luggage so I can live out what my mind has imagined over the last few months. Les reaches in my direction...but...not...for...me. He reaches for my luggage and whispers, "We can't hug or kiss." Well, my heart dropped to my toes and took about five minutes before it decided to get back to its original state. LOL. The walk to our driver was the longest walk in life. I had to remember that I was going to be with him for a month. Needless to say I quickly became accustomed to the cultural differences on many levels. The first one was "no touchy touchy feely feely".

Everyone who knew I was coming prepared gifts for me. If they were unaware then they made sure the next time they saw me they had a gift or were able to cater to me in some form. Just think, I was nervous traveling to the Middle East because of the imagery provided by the media. Little did I know that I would have the time of my life and meet people who would forever be my friends. I quickly found that true friendship is not based on the time you've known someone but in the quality of what is mutually invested that makes it true and pure. I had no idea that my closest friends would be found in a distant land but at the end of the day it's God's plan and we never know what he has cooking.

Ok. So here's some juice. After being dropped off by our driver, Les and I enter his flat and I immediately feel at home. We drop my luggage, quickly embrace each other, and give each other a kiss that was four months in waiting. I couldn't wait to feel his arms wrapped around my body. The strength of his arms and the warmth of his body allowed me to melt into a state of rhapsody. Chile, all I saw was shooting stars, fireworks, and... Ok now y'all know I ain't telling all the juice. What happens with Les...stays with Les. But I will tell you that it was well worth the wait. There are somethings face time just can't handle. But after some much needed lover's time he took me out for a night on the town. I had the opportunity to finally see the beauty, culture, and the night life in Abu Khali. Venue after venue, acquaintance after acquaintance, I realized that this country thousands of miles from home was safely harboring my baby and I felt that same safety immediately. It was as if the media lied about what the Middle East represented. Nowhere did I see disparity and I felt safer in Abu Khali then I did in the good ole U.S of A. Police officers don't carry guns. Citizens don't carry guns, and everyone greets each other with peace. Alcohol is completely controlled, and drugs are nonexistent. The homeless are rarely seen but they are taken care of by the community which minimizes anyone being in complete lack leaving no reason to victimize other people. Things to ponder.

Fast forward. Les took me to one of the clubs that he manages called Cuba Cubana. When we arrived there were floods of people waiting to enter. It was if the United Nations decided to have a celebration. There were people from all over the world. Bouncers lined the entrance from the beginning of the red carpet to the main entrance of the posh club. Valet parked our car and we entered via the VIP entrance. A mahogany door opened to a colorful and chic room filled with red and blue plush velvet chairs, warm flashing lights, enchanting candles burning, staff uniformed and ready to serve. Our table was reserved for a party of twelve. As soon as we were seated our waiter appeared with the house wine. Soon after, the doors opened and the crowd rushed in with a magnetic excitement. Women entered with unzipped black ajabas allowing their high-end club attire that screamed, "I am sexy!", to be seen through the smoke-filled walls of Cuba Cubana where Europe, New York, Vegas, Abu Khali, and Saudi Arabia all merged. Rumor has it "what happens in Cuba Cubana...stays in Cuba Cubana". Five more couples joined Les and I at our table. One by one I was introduced. Each encounter was filled with excitement and they all spoke as if they had known me for years. The crazier thing was the gifts just kept on giving. Perfume, cashmere scarves, jewelry, gift cards, desserts, and the list goes on and on. I should have brought an extra suitcase. I was truly overwhelmed with the continued hospitality. Les should have warned me. But, I don't think he knew that this particular night we'd be calling for an extra car to take my gifts back to the flat. Anyways, the couples. That night I met Jazmina and Orlando, Nafisa and Mohammed, Ngoyo and Benti, Tao and Khalif, and Treese and Stephanie.

Jazmina and Orlando are a boyfriend girlfriend duo who are contracted to be in Abu Khali as local performers. They bring the spice and sexy of South America to the Middle East. Nafisa and Mohammed are married, they have a son, and they are both natives of Abu Khali. Nafisa is a master percussionist and Mohammed runs his family printing company. Ngoyo and Benti are "just friends." Benti is a biochemist and Ngoyo is still trying to establish herself in Abu Khali. Tao and Khalif are newly engaged. Tao is a personal trainer contracted in Abu Khali and Khalif is a well-known drummer from Dubai. Last but not least we have Treese and Stephanie. Treese is an officer in the United States Navy stationed in Abu Khali for 2 years. Stephanie is a registered nurse visiting from Australia. Treese and Stephanie have been partners for two years. Throughout the time I stayed in Abu Khali I had the opportunity to get to know these awesome people. We would double date, have dinners, shop, go sightseeing, and just simply hang out. One of our most exciting double dating excursions was when the "Mighty 12", my nickname for the crew, decided to go to a cookout in the desert. I have never in my life imagined driving through the desert let alone at night. The terrain was bumpy and clearly not paved for regular automobiles. We rode out in SUVs around 8:30 pm. We went from tall skyscrapers and illuminated highways to a deserted desert where snakes, spiders, and other desert creatures were the majority.

We arrived at a military style campground where tents were pitched for miles. Each section was privately owned and gated with traditional bob wire fencing. The gate was manually opened by Saladin, Les' friend who was a sergeant in the Abu Khali Army. When we exited our SUVs we were greeted by other co-owners. To my surprise the inside of the tents were weather proofed, fully furnished with living room furniture and flat screen televisions, video games, surround sound, DJ equipment, and a pool table.

Of course you know I had to ask for the restroom because I've never used the restroom in the desert before and I needed to know what I was up against because my first experience in using a public restroom in Abu Khali had been more than eventful. Les and I went to the gym one day. Before going I prepared a green superfood smoothie to nourish our bodies for the intense workout we planned on having. After a few hours of my intense cardio, core strengthening, and two games of one on one basketball my stomach was in an uproar. I ran out that gym faster than the road runner from looney tunes. I rushed into the bathroom, found the first empty stall and you know what. Before I went in I looked for paper towels and there was none. There was only a motion sensor hand dryer. I figured they'd have seat covers inside the stall, but they didn't. I was left to my own devices and memory recall allowed me to just do what ladies do and hope for the best for my hip and thigh muscles. Man, the burn was real, but it was finally over. So, I looked to my left then to my right and neither direction presented toilet paper. I was a dear stuck in headlights when I realized I couldn't clean myself off. I yelled out an embarrassing, "Hello", but I was the only one in the bathroom. I looked again just to make sure I didn't overlook any present toilet paper. To my left there was a ray of hope but it would be a challenge. There was a shiny silver shataff (bidet) or hose as we know it in western culture. It would be my first time using it and I wasn't quite sure how to maneuver. I didn't want to get my clothing wet, so I strategically removed my clothing from the waist down. The time of reckoning had come. I grabbed the shataff, sprayed the areas that needed cleaning, prayed that it had the same effect as toilet paper and wipes, and placed it back on the holder. I was dripping wet but i had to make a mad dash to see if there was anything I could test the application with. I peeped out of the stall, said my little "hello", darted for the sink that was holding a stack of paper towels, ran back into the stall and redeemed myself. So now you see why I had to take a look at the amenities at the campground. Stop laughing at me...LOL.

One of the owners walked me to what was the Mercedes Benz of porta potties. The outside was black with chrome finish. When he opened the door for me, I felt like I walked into a million-dollar bathroom. It was absolutely gorgeous with its marble countertop, chrome toilet, chrome sink, chrome faucets with hot water, cherry wood flooring, recessed lighting, a chrome shataff, and TOILET PAPER!!!!!!! Sold! Now back to the cookout.

They had prepared a feast out of this world. The menu for the evening consisted of unlimited crabs, grilled and fried fish, rice, and salad. The meat was cooked in a pit dug out the sand and wood causing the fire to burn like a bonfire. We sat on blankets and pillows and ate our hearts out. We laughed, joked, played games, and simply enjoyed the peace that only the desert and good friends could bring. While the guys bonded so did the ladies. That night the windows of our souls started to open and our sisterhood made an oath to build and hold each other up. Six different women from all walks of life proved that sisterhood transcends race, religion, creed, sexual preference, politics, and socio-economic status. We realized that night that we were all beautiful and toxic at the same damn time.

GIRLS NIGHT OUT

A chorus of waiters and restaurant staff start to move about Cuba Cubana preparing for the anticipated crowd for the night. Arab music plays as Hanifa is behind the bar setting the glasses in place and wiping down the counter. Each waiter goes about their nightly prep but they are all moved to speak at the same time.

"It's the weekend. Just got paid. Friday Night. Person after person flooding the dance floor. Getting away from the hustle and bustle of the week. Abu Khali is the place to be. It's pretty much like your Las Vegas. Accept there's not a lot of glitz. Not a lot of color but when you step inside Cuba Cubana the world is full of color. People come from all over. Saudi Arabia, Dubai, Europe, Africa, Asia, and the Americas. You name it they are here. A great melting pot. International DJ's...hit after hit...the best live entertainment in the United Emirates. Oh boy here comes Hanifa."

Hanifa walks between the guys. She lifts the bar ledge so she can get to the other side.

"Ummmm. Hello. You forgot to mention the best drinks in the region! People come to Relax...Relate...Release... I am the queen of the three

R's. They should put a PHD after my name cause one good one and momma gets all the info. I help folk compartmentalize the "stuff" they deal with on a regular basis?"

A couple walks in going to a table.

"OK, see that couple over there? That's Lori and Suliman. Married for five years. He's an engineer and she's a school teacher. Both expats. She can't stand it here. She's always complaining about going home, being home sick, the heat, and Chile she can't stand covering. Suliman on the other hand, on the low, likes to hang out at the afterhours 'cause he can't stand going home. Drama...ok. And he is the biggest flirt. Every Friday he cuts up. He tried it with me and you know I put him in his place 'cause I don't do married men. Plus….my Boo Ahmed is right there. Just thought I'd drop that just in case any of you had your eye on him."

Hanifa continues setting the bar while the chorus continues.

"You never know who you're going to meet when you walk through the doors of Cuba Cubana. Sexy ladies dressed in the finest fashion, brothers GQ from head to toe. Princes, ambassadors, owners of fortune 500 companies, military personnel, celebrities, and the chicest of the chic. Once they walk through the door everyone is the same. Different name just escaping. Dressed to escape. Dancing to escape. Drinking to escape. Flirting to escape. Escape what? Reality. Yup, Reality. Stress, hurt, baby daddy drama. You name it...they got it. We're just here to serve and make their escape as memorable as possible. Not to mention the money in Abu Khali is three times the currency from other countries. As a matter of fact, none of the employees here are "citizens". You want quick money...good money...get a sponsor and come to Abu Khali. Opening time! Opening time! 1 Minute to go. Money time. Party time. Baby let's go! They're lining up. Let's go baby. Doors opening in 5, 4, 3, 2,1."

The DJ starts to play unforgettable by French Montana. Security is checking id's and assessing the crowd. The party goers are dressed in trendy and chic clothing. Cuba Cubana has opened for business! Free, Tao, Treese, Ngoyo, Jasmina, and Hanifa enter. The flashing lights, the base, and energy from the party goers add excitement as the girlfriends walk up to the bouncer. The bouncer checks their id's with a very stern disposition making the party goers understand that nonsense will not be tolerated. The ladies enter one by one onto the dance floor.

Drake's song Unforgettable is playing and all club patrons start dancing. Free immediately loses herself in the music and starts daydreaming. She's back home at a poetry slam at Rock and Chews Lounge. She has on an African print skirt, jean jacket, a pair of Dr. Martin boots, and a hat. The crowd snaps their fingers as she takes the microphone.

"Unforgettable huh? Actually, yeah... I am unforgettable. I mean I'm deeper than the pots your momma fries her chicken in. I've cruised through your mind while you were sleeping. Controlling your dreams and making you taste the sweetness of my estrogen beads as they evaporate on your chin. I'm the Sheba to your Solomon. The scarlet in your hemoglobin. Your best friend. Sometimes bruised but I fix it up for you. Joy when nobody's watching...sorrow when nobody sees me crying. Cascading tears mixing with rose colored blush...I blush for you...hold it together for you...for me. Toxic and beautiful at the same damn time. Unable to press rewind and redo all that's been done. But when I recognize its me and the sun and we have no choice but to work out the trauma, bad intentions, hurts, pains, scars and cover up with everything society says is right, acceptable, status quo...beautiful."

Ngoyo taps Free on the shoulder and motions her to return to the group. They resume dancing to the regular tempo of Unforgettable. A waiter is setting up their table. They make their way to the table and take their seats. Ahmed, the head waiter, makes his way stoically to the VIP table where Free, Tao, Ngoyo, Treese, Jazmina, and Nafisa are sitting. Ngoyo notices him and immediately goes into flirtation mode fixing her breasts and glossing her lips.

"Good evening ladies. My name is Ahmed and I'll be your server. I have to let you know that tonight is lady's night. Drinks are free and appetizers are half price."

Free, excited and full of a celebratory spirit responds.

"Yes baby. Tonight has my name all over it. I didn't know it was lady's night. I didn't see it advertised online."

She starts dancing in her seat as if she's heard her favorite song and Ahmed laughs.

"Management just started the promotion this week so you are right on time.

Here are the menus. I'll give you a few moments to look over the specials and I'll be back to take your order."

All of the ladies respond with a gracious thank you. Ngoyo watches him as he walks away then rolls her eyes in her head then belts,

"He is cute! Chile. I might have met my husband." Tao laughs and adjusts the straps on her dress. She pulls out a compact mirror to check her lip stick which is painted on to perfection.

"Everywhere we go you always think you've found your husband and you never marry nobody."

Nafisa interjects sarcastically.

"Maybe you should wait for Allah to send you your husband. Let him bring a dowry that will be worth you considering marriage. Not every man is husband material. What do you think Jazmina?"

"Well, I agree with Nafisa but on the other hand maybe God sends her places where she can potentially meet her husband. You never know where you might receive your blessing."

Ahmed walks back over to the ladies smoothly stepping to what the DJ is spinning. He has an Ipad in tote.

"Ok ladies. Are we ready to order?"

One by one they give their selections.

"Yes, I'd like to have the purple kiss and an order of calamari and an order of honey barbeque wings."

"I'll take the tsunami and a chicken Caesar salad."

"I'm not really hungry so I'll just get two pink lollipops."

"I'll take an order of calamari and a ginger ale."

21

"Can I have the wings and a ginger ale?"
Ahmed nods his head and turns his attention to Ngoyo.

"And what would you like pretty lady?"
With every piece of ratchet-ness in her veins Ngoyo blurts out...

"Y'all being all prissy. Ahmed, I'd like everything on the menu and 4 Long Island Iced teas."
Everyone in complete shock drops their jaws.
"4?!"
"I don't want to have to carry you out before the party is over little lady."
"You can carry me anytime Mr. Ahmed and I don't mind changing my name to whatever your last name is honey."
"That's an honor. So, would that be all ladies?
"Yes."
Ahmed nods then gestures to Ngoyo.

"OK. That's one long island iced tea for you little lady?"
"For now. Keep my tab open. I might want to add you to it."
Ngoyo winks at Ahmed as he walks away laughing but throwing a flirtatious wink at her. Free is playfully annoyed.

"I can't take you anywhere. Damn. Let that man breath."
"Girl, I will give him all the breath he needs for life."
Ngoyo takes a long deep breath and acts like she is performing CPR. She throws her legs in the air and whispers loudly.

"Come to momma now that you got your life back. I got nine lives for baby."

Jazmina focuses her attention on the dance floor. She is relieved to finally have a night off and not be the performer.

"I get to let my hair down and relax. You have no idea how much I needed this girl's night. I literally work 6 days a week and I need some "me" time."

Nafisa and Ngoyo chime in.

"Me time? What's that?

"Ummmm...that's when you...get to spend time with yourself...so that you don't worry about the husband, the kids, the family, the job, the cooking, the cleaning, the bills, the homework, the doctor's appointments, the-

The ladies clearly wanting her to shut up," Ngoyo We get it!" Ngoyo continues as if she has just given her dissertation.

"Well good cause Me Myself and I are about to go and light fire on that dance floor tonight Baby!"

She prances onto the dance floor followed by the rest of the girls. The DJ decided that he would pull from his disco and house music playlists. While he was spinning, he inserted Michael Jackson's "Off The Wall" and the crowd went crazy. A video of Michael's live performance played on the projector as people felt like they were in his presence. Two dancers covered in body art danced on a six-foot-tall platform as bubbles floated around them.

In the middle of the floor were two Middle Eastern women dressed in black. The first was about five feet eleven inches in height. Her hair was silky black and reached her tail bone. The disco ball reflected on her cherry red bottom Fendi stilettos as her ajaba coasted along the dance floor. Her counterpart was about five feet five inches tall wearing a

black knee length bubble Gucci dress. She toted a slim cigarette as she lost herself in the music. The two of them seemed to be entranced and moved in slow motion while the other 200 patrons attempted their best Michael Jackson moves. They switched from partner to partner after every chorus making sure that no one danced alone. But somehow the two mysterious women remained totally disengaged. It was as if they were being guided by a spiritual entity that wanted them to experience the music from a hallucinogenic and outer body perspective. It was as if they were trying to savor every ounce of music, good vibes, and freedom they could experience before it was time to go back to their reality. They traveled an hour and forty- five minutes from Saudi Arabia. A place where women are the lesser than and where extreme Sharia law is enforced. If the Mutawa or religious police were to see them they could possibly be punished under religious law. So, this was there moment of escape, freedom, individuality, and self-absorption. While everyone else moved to the rhythm and tempo of the song these two women moved in ultra-slow motion as if they were dancing to a three hour you tube chakra meditation track at a yoga retreat.

That's pretty much how the rest of the evening went. Of course, there was girl talk and releasing but the next plan was for las seis amigas to go to Al Hadi Retreat and Day Spa while the guys planned their next basketball tournament. I know you're probably wondering why I'm not spending more time with Les. Trust me, I didn't come this far not to be with my bae. There is twenty-four hours in a day...trust we had our Tank and Adina Howard moments. Wait...did I just say that? LOL. Ok...let's get to the retreat.

24

RETREAT

Google's definition of retreat: (verb) 1. Withdraw from enemy forces as a result of their superior power or after defeat; (noun) 1. An act of moving back or withdrawing; 2. A signal for a military force to withdraw.

The girls decided to go to a day spa where they can relax. When they walk in they are immediately captivated by the serenity. The smell of rosemary smothered the atmosphere. The sounds of waterfall and soothing meditation music hypnotized them as the hostess greeted them knowing them each by name. They are whisked back to the changing room where each of the ladies is assigned a locker containing a plush robe, slippers, and towel. They change into their robes and one by one they are lead into the transition room where they have their feet soaked in aroma therapy of their choice. They are served mimosas, wine, lemon water, and fruit during their wait. Each lady is assigned a masseuse, an esthetician to perform a facial, and a private Turkish bath. Between each session they all reconvene in the brine room which is beautifully decorated with a wall length waterfall, beach style chairs with brown comforters to keep their bodies warm between services, a wet bar with drinks of their choice, and relaxing halogen lightening that changed the mood of the room every three minutes. Pink to remind them of their compassion, love, hope, good spirits, health, and wellbeing. Blue to remind them of the depth of their trust, wisdom, and royalty. Yellow to remind them of the need for clarity and understanding.

The brine room was a place of quiet stillness where you are able to meditate, gain clarity, calm your spirit, assess your life, or simply just exist in the moment. While there, they are overcome with a degree of self-awareness that was absent for quite some time. The becoming one with yourself experience gripped all of them so much so that they were able to rid themselves of the cares and stress of the world even if it was for just a few hours. One by one they began to cry as self-realization and releasing guided them. One by one they began to journey through their lives. Recalling joys, pains, victories, defeats, trauma, and overcoming. They went back to the eye of the storm:

Eye of The Storm

Sunny day... kids playing hopscotch, double dutch, tops, and catch a girl get a girl. My side of the street don't have no shade so the heat is baking my cocoa skin Across the street...tree lined, shade, cool, and peace and it's only 20 feet away.

I see the storm coming. Dark clouds eclipse the sun on my side but the shade and sun never touch across the street.

Everybody looking saying how crazy it is...they think it's the end of the world cause stuff like that only happen on tv. Yup 3, 6, 10, 12, 17, 29, and 57...Floor model...Modeling, prancing, playing and it's starting to drizzle. But, only on my side. Thunder screams and demands attention.

Showers streaming, puddles catching each H_2O component casting two Hydrogen particles and one Oxygen.
One takes life and the other the source of life but they dwell together in harmony. How so? How amazing?
Balance...Circle of life...Giver of life...water.
Taker of life is the O element missing in action while the storm is
coming and I'm caught in the eye of the storm.
Everyone runs for cover across the street but i never get permission so I get drenched in the rain.
Lightning flashes before me almost touching my skin but I was
protected on all sides…
Flower child...daddy's little girl...drenched by the sun's protection even in
the midst of chaos.
No signs of being beaten by the storm so it's assumed that I was always ok. Internalizing each storm and coping by just moving on but
what nobody realized was that the storms never moved on in my mind
but my soul fought for healing and it wins every time!

THE JEWEL OF SOUTH AMERICA

Cartagena, Colombia 2009

The streets are filled with the vibrant colors of Carnival. Salsa, merengue, bachata, and afro Latin music saturates the city as visitors and natives' parade through the streets of Cartagena in vibrant and spiritual costumes...mix of santeria, erotica, and freedom. At the main stage the attendees are waiting in anticipation for the local and international artists that will grace the stage. Jazmina is off stage talking to her little boy while her band prepares to load in. She gives Juaquin a motherly kiss on the forehead then hands him his favorite transformer. Her sister takes his hand and takes him to the front of the stage. The host energizes the crowd and announces Jazmina. The band starts to play. A beautiful Latina dances her way onto the stage in a purple diamond studded dress with fringed ends, three-inch purple and diamond studded heels, flowing jet black hair, and her face flawlessly made. Her dancers followed her with spicy Latin flavor. They were magnetic and set the stage on fire. Jazmina truly represented the heart and soul of Colombia.

She had been dancing and singing since she was five years old. Her parents paid her way through the performing arts University in the area and she acquired a bachelor of arts degree. Not only was she a phenomenal singer and dancer, but she mastered the saxophone as well. A true star who was a cross between Shakira, Beyonce, and Sheila E. So much so that a local promoter and musician by the name of Orlando Sanchez offered the opportunity to travel with him to the UAE. This small town girl now had the opportunity of her life time. Jazmina dreamed of traveling the world performing in stadiums and flying from country to country. She was destined to be an international sensation and Orlando was the key to her dreams coming true. They talked for about a week over the phone. A month later Orlando invited Jazmina to his music studio. It was filled with hi tech recording equipment, instruments, and a chic recording room that literally melted her heart away. It was a singer's dream studio. He walked her into the booth, arranged the mic, dimmed the lights and walked away. He sat at the engineer's booth flicked a few switches and chose a track for Jazmina. As soon as the music started she felt like she was in heaven. Melody's flowed from her lips and for the first time ever Jazmina and Orlando made magic together. Their chemistry was magnetic, so they quickly became a couple.

What Jazmina didn't know was that Orlando was a runner for a local cartel and he was living a double life. Orlando was introduced to the drug game when he was only ten years old. His uncle Raul would use him to transport narcotics in his book bag because the authorities wouldn't suspect a child would be transporting drugs worth one hundred thousand pesos weekly. His payout from his uncle was always the best toys, clothing, and money. This continued into his teenage years. When he turned 21 his uncle put him in charge of handling the finances for the local cartel. Business was seamless for a while but eventually the game caught up to him. Orlando couldn't account for over two million pesos and he had to relocate immediately because there was a bounty out on him. So, he convinced Jazmina to leave much sooner than they had discussed.

The day had come when Jazmina had to say goodbye to her baby. She would be relocating to Abu Khali as a contracted performer and would stay there for 10 months out of the year. Leaving Juaquin and her family was the most difficult thing she's had to do in her life. But she was leaving to create a better life for him.

Abu Khali 2017

"Eight years I've been here in Abu Khali. I came here to make money to sustain my family. My baby is 14 years. Every time I talk to him I just want to pinch his cheeks and hold him in my arms. Wait a minute...I actually have his picture for you to see.

She pulls out her cellphone and shows a picture of her son. Jazmina gazes into the phone as if she's daydreaming.

"My baby. I sacrifice for my baby every day. I've come 13,000 miles to create a life for him only to see him two months out of the year. I came to Abu Khali with Orlando to have a good music career and for him to get out of the cartel. So, we came together. Business is always good but the more popular I get, the more men come to show their appreciation, and the more time I spend with my girlfriends the more jealous he gets. I try to show him that he has nothing to worry about but my words mean nothing. Two years ago, he started drinking really heavy. He started getting really depressed and he tried to kill himself and he stabbed me. We tried to keep it quiet because the island is really small but people talk. I thought about leaving but if I did I would've lost everything. So, I stayed and just prayed that he would change. That life would get better. But it hasn't. It's gotten worse. He's drinking every night. I found out he was cheating on me so I stopped having sex with him so he is now very angry at me. Because I won't have sex with him he breaks the door to my bedroom to get in and I act like I am sleeping so he will leave me alone. But, he falls to sleep. If he sees me talking to another man he goes on drinking and does things that he doesn't remember the next day. Last night I was leaving Cuba Cubana and he ran me off the road. I was scared for my life. Free and Les saw it and ran to my rescue. I cried in Free's arms and prayed that God would save me. He's had two car accidents this month and he's facing possible jail time if any more accidents occur while driving drunk. His visa is in jeopardy and our employer can be fined if he does jail time. When your life revolves around your relationship and your business it's difficult to just leave. I pray and pray. I try to let him see that he's sabotaging what we've spent years to build. He sees it but he's on a vicious cycle. So, until I figure it out I'll just escape every once in a while with my girls and keep my baby boy close to my heart cause after all...This is for him."

PROTECT AND SERVE

Abu Khali, US Naval Base. September 2015

Treese is walking down the street after detail duty. It's 11:30 pm and she is headed back to her apartment. The streets are pretty dark with only light from the buildings that line the cold military base street. As a naval officer she's trained to be on guard so she scopes the area while she maintains her stride. Out of the darkness she hears a faint "hey baby". Her senses heighten because no one is visible. At one point she thought maybe her mind was playing tricks on her but then the faint voice transitioned into a physical presence. A tall male standing about six feet appears three steps behind her. She picks up her pace and begins to calculate her defense as his footsteps enclose. A head of her is her apartment about two thousand feet. To her left is the street and the library which closed four hours ago. To her right is an alley and the chapel. The stalker grabs her from behind in trained military fashion making it impossible for her to defend herself. He shoves a cloth in her mouth and begins to threaten her as he pulls her into the alley. Gleaming from the chapel are images of Christ outstretching his hands. As tears fall from her eyes, angels and cherubs holding horns shout sounds of tragedy and defeat.

"I don't have freedom! Everyday I'm locked in the memory of "Hey baby, Yo! Shawty! Let me holla at you! Following me 2 blocks with uncomfortable barks of untamed masculine vernacular. Like, what the fuck! Leave Me Alone! Even when I started walking faster he paced faster grabbing my arm. I tried to snatch away and run but his grip was too tight. I struggled to break free but his strength grew with every resistance. He pulled me into a staircase shoving his scarf in my mouth. I screamed and cried but my muffled yell for help didn't stop him. The kiss of a stranger on my neck was like an angry pit bull gnawing on my flesh. Each release of saliva nauseated me. I wish to God I had worn pants. My skirt made it easy for him to rip my panties and force his penis inside of me. Each thrust was like a knife to my womanhood! My tears were the loudest cries from my soul. After he ejaculated in me he rested his demonic flesh on me as if he'd experienced euphoria. Then he jumped up, fixed his pants, whispered his sympathy, and ran away taking my soul with him."

Treese decided to go into the military because her father was her hero. He served in the military for 20 years. He was wounded in battle when his troop was ambushed in Kuwait. He suffered a gunshot wound to the head and had to get a metal plate placed. Over the years he has struggled with memory loss and an acute onset of Parkinson's disease that severely debilitated him. He also suffers from PTSD which has affected his daily living.

Treese has done one tour of duty and engaged in battle. She also suffers from PTSD as well because of her seeing her friend shot, the pain her family experienced because of her father's PTSD episodes, and her rape. Over the years she's sought counseling and is currently able to live a normal life without many episodes.

Abu Khali 2017

Treese met Stephanie the first year she was stationed in Abu Khali. Treese was invited to a New Year's Eve party hosted by the US ambassador. There were people from different professions at this all access extravaganza. Military, politicians, business owners, musicians, athletes, doctors, you name it they were there. It was a sexy illusive scene out of a James Bond movie. Treese walked almost in slow motion toward the cash bar. Every few steps she would stop and taste one of the delicious appetizers being served. At her last reach another hand went for the same stuffed salmon bite. Neither hand touched the salmon but the fingers of two strangers touched one another mid stride. A tall Caucasian woman with a short blonde pixie cut and hazel eyes stared Treese in the eyes with an embarrassing grin. They both gestured to the other signaling the cue to oblige and take what was left. They performed a verbal tango of kind words to each other as the waiter walked away with the tray. Stephanie spoke in a soft yet assertive Australian accent which peaked Treese's curiosity. The two began to chat and by the end of the evening they were like the best of friends. They retired to Stephanie's flat since Treese had a weekend pass. That night they learned more about each other opening Pandora's box of intrigue, sisterhood, and lust. That night they made love in their own way, in their own time, and woke up in the morning with no regrets. Stephanie has been by Treese's side ever since. Treese has 4 more years left in the military. When she retires, they plan on moving back to the USA to get married. But while they are in Abu Khali they can't let it be known that they are lesbians. If found out in public, they could both endure Sharia law regarding homosexuality.

LIVING BEYOND RACE

Houston General Hospital 1983

A scream permeates the halls of the prenatal unit.
The door opens to a room where Lang Li is giving birth while Roderick stands there holding her hand as the team escorts Tao into the world. The love they have for each other is felt intensely.

Her head comes out first. Her crown is jet black, her skin is tanned, and her cry demands attention. Lang Li cries when she holds her baby girl in her arms and Roderick smiles as only a father can when he sees his baby girl for the first time.

"Look at my baby girl! Wow! I can't believe we made her Babe!"

Roderick is disbelief in how beautiful his baby girl is. Tears of joy stream from the couple as the nurse places her in her mother's arms pressing her firmly against her breasts.

Boston, Massachusetts 1993

Ten years later Tao is on her way home from school walking with her schoolmates. A car drives by with a group of Italian teenagers screaming out of the window.

"It's bad enough we got niggers moving in! Go back to China ching chong!"

The driver throws a bottle of bleach into the crowd splattering bleach over their school uniforms. They all stand in disbelief looking at their clothes, each other, and the fleeing car. Tao breaks out into silent tears.

Thailand 1999

Tao is on summer break with her family in Thailand. She pulls in front of her grandmother's home. Family members come to greet her. She's in the car full of nervousness and excitement. This is her first time in Thailand and she prayed that it would be a good experience since her mother and father spoke so much about it. Her father opened the back door for her to exit. As she stepped out the children began to laugh and point. Her cousin Phan walks over and touches her hair then runs back to others screaming and flailing her arms. In Thai she screamed,

"Darkie! Darkie! Can't come to the party. Take off some skin so you can blend because black is bad like sin!"

The rest of the family stood in shock at the fact that Tao was darker than they were and the fact that Phan had just embarrassed the entire family. Roderick pulled Lang Lin aside to be debriefed on what was going on. When she translated what they were saying Roderick made the decision to stay at a hotel for their stay. He made it a point that the only people welcomed to come visit them or be around them were those who authentically wanted to get to know him and Tao, and who welcomed them into the family.

For years Tao would have to endure discrimination from her own family and the rest of the world. Regardless of how exotic she looked she suffers constantly.

Abu Khali 2017

Since I've been in Abu Khali a few clubs and other establishments won't let me in because Abu Khali has a heavy population of Asian prostitutes. You never see them in the streets because it's illegal. Certain clubs refuse access to my Asian sisters because they automatically assume that if you're Asian you're a jump off!". On the low, prostitution boosts the economy in the hotel industry. My heart bleeds because I know some of them didn't have a choice.

It's a blessing and a curse. My entire life I've had to deal with the questions and the stereotypes. Questions like, "what are you and where are you from?" Like, I'm a biracial human. Half Black Half Thai. But, what difference does it make? Why can't I just identify as "ME". Growing up was such a struggle. I was teased as a child. I was called every racial slur that could be said about Asians. It was so bad that I would try to color my skin brown so my black friends would stop picking on me. When I would visit my mother's family in Thailand I would be treated different because my skin was darker, my hair was curly, and because I wasn't "pure" Thai. Imagine the trauma a child suffers when they feel like they don't belong because of the color of their skin or because of their physical features. I deal with that crap whenever I meet someone new. Same line of questioning and I'm sick of it! When I go out with my friends, security assumes that I am a prostitute because of my features. Damn! When is enough, enough? I want to be free of offense and I want people to accept me for me!

MIDDLE EAST PULSATIONS

Abu Khali 2010

A drove of women enter into a two-story building with a heightened sense of urgency. Some are dressed in all black ajabas all adorned with either exquisite black jewels, embroidery, lace, silk, or designs. From the second-floor windows, splashes of lighted flashed multi-colored strobes as if they were suggesting Al Maasuq was going to be the hot spot for the evening. There was some truth to the language of the lights. Just below the awning of the front entrance was a life-sized poster of Nafisa standing next to a set of Latin percussion covered in rhinestones. Nafisa (Master Percussionist) was the headliner for the evening wooing audiences from every town in Abu Khali. The synergy was unreal. Nafisa was the women's champion because she dominated a skill that was originally dominated by men. She was taught by her father as a child and nurtured her craft even when it was undesirable for a woman to play. The heart and sound of the drums was her peace.

That night Nafisa was being honored by the Ministry of the Arts. She received a key to the country by Prince Sadiq Al Iman which was the highest honor any musician in Abu

Khali could receive. Especially a woman. In a room full of women who eagerly awaited her entry, Nafisa emerged through satin covered drapery dressed in a white and gold Louis Vuitton ajaba handmade especially for her. As she cascaded down the walkway the crowd gave her a standing ovation and photographers scurried to get "the picture of the year". The supporting musicians begin to play her hit song and the crowd erupts again. Nafisa takes her place and begins to breathe life into the congos.

Abu Khali 2015

The Nikah. Nafisa and Mohammed's wedding ceremony. This was the day everyone was waiting for. They chose to have the ceremony at his family's mansion. The outer court was decorated by Bahiya El Madin, the event planner for the elite in Abu Khali. It was a wedding fit for a queen. The women sat surrounding Nafisa and the men sat surrounding Mohammed. There were two chairs specifically for the bride and groom and the Imam stood between them.

Islamic law suggests that the Imam explain the purpose of marriage and guide a couple to the best ways of maintaining their union. In the midst of family and friends, the newlywed couple acknowledged their understanding of the marriage covenant. They vowed to live in unity and righteousness. They were excited to begin their journey and to live out their duties to one another. Nafisa was excited to become a wife and a mother. But, what she didn't know was that life would change in many ways.

"As-salaam- alaikum. Yes. It's 11 pm. Yes, I know. I lost track of time. No, I didn't go anywhere else. What? Another man? Where did you get that from? I don't want another man. Call the authorities for what? I haven't done anything. What are you talking about? Hello. Hello...Hello.

The phone hangs up on the other end. She slowly puts her phone away.

"He does this all the time. The moment something is not to his liking or if he thinks that I'm getting too worldy he threatens to accuse me of adultery which carries an automatic five year prison term here unless I can find three men who can attest that I am wholesome and such an act is not in my character. The last time he did it I had to call for my father, my uncle, and my brother to come and stand as witnesses for me. He doesn't realize that his jealousy can cause me to lose everything...my child, my job, and my reputation. I married because my father arranged our union with my husband's father. There was no attraction or connection in the beginning but after our marriage I learned to love him the way a wife is supposed to love her husband. There are times when I just want to run away but I can't. If I leave, I automatically forfeit my child over to him. I never told anyone but when I cut my hair, he beat me. He said a woman is to never cut their hair...it is a sign of beauty and womanhood. He told me that I looked like a lesbian and that anything that looked like haram would bring attention to me...to us.

In everyone's eyes we are the perfect couple. But every night before I go to sleep I pray that Allah would remove him from my life...don't kill him...just remove him so that I can have a chance at being free. I am a master percussionist but I haven't played in over 5 years because he won't allow me. So every time I get the opportunity hear the beat of the drum, rhythms, and music it's worth the risk."

DISPLACED AFRICAN DIAMOND

Nairobi Kenya. June 1980

Ngoyo is having lunch with her family at their compound on a beautiful Sunday afternoon after church. Her mother has the house smelling delicious. The dining room table is covered with food and Ngoyo's mouth is watering as they start to prepare their plates with ugali, mushrooms, fish stew, and matoke. Gunmen invade Ngoyo's family compound.

"They killed my father when I was 15. The rebels found where we were staying and destroyed our home. I was sitting at the breakfast table waiting for my mother to come downstairs and take me to school. As she was coming down the stairs they kicked in the door, threw tear gas through the window, and burst in snatching my mother and me. A man lifted his shotgun and pointed in my father's direction shooting him in the head. They poured petroleum over our home and lit a torch. My mother and I tried to save my father but...there were no saving him. They left us for dead.

By the grace of God, we escaped what used to be our home and fled to the US to live with my uncle. He took very good care of us. Almost as good as my father. The only difference was that his way of receiving gratitude from me was by having sex. He molested me until I was old enough to leave. I told my mother but of course she took his word over mine because our tradition gives the man the honor of truth when accused. They said I had no right enticing him. I lost my father and then I lost my mother to war, tradition, and a lie."

Abu Khali 2017

I try to love, I try to trust, I try to show my pure authentic self but the walls I've built hold me hostage. I flirt with love but then I run. I have images of falling in love with the right one but then I question my stability and ability to love through PTSD. I've ran all the way to Abu Khali to find freedom. I know the road to freedom is finding closure but how can I if I haven't faced my demons, my hurt, my grief. I can't imagine letting anyone in right now but I guess I'm at a good start with my girls."

FRIENDSHIP

After hearing the stories from Treese, Tao, Ngoyo, Nafisa, and Jazmina I knew that we were all purposed to become friends. I was honored that they trusted me enough, a stranger, to share their journeys and innermost secrets with. We laughed, we cried, we prayed, and we released toxins from our bodies and our minds. It felt good to just release...to retreat.

We realized that we hold on to years of trauma and hurt and never allow ourselves to be freed up from those toxins. But when we meet other people who have similar stories or those we can relate to in some degree, triggers prompt us to acknowledge the pain. Once we acknowledge it's important to share how it has made us feel or how it has impacted our lives. The next step is to forgive. This may be the most difficult part of releasing. We are at the point of consciously and willingly forgiving those who have hurt us or even forgiving ourselves for hurting ourselves and others. Forgiveness is you no longer holding people hostage in your mind or no longer giving them power over you...power they don't even know they have.

Once we cross the threshold of forgiveness, we can then begin our journey to restoration. We look toward the future by calling out those things that will give us the life we desire. We actually created vision boards. We each created a board that consisted of inspirational quotes, pictures of our dream houses, jobs, trips, weddings, and etc... Your vision board is limitless just like your dreams. But, in order to accomplish and maintain your vision you need accountability. We made a pact to communicate with each other once a month on our progress, our hang ups, frustrations, and anything associated with our continuous journey to being whole and walking in our true beauty. We realized we had something special. We had that Sex in The City and Girlfriends type of bond and we promised to always be our sister's keeper 'cause we can't walk this thing alone.

QUIET TIME

OK...so...in all of my ripping and running and learning the lives of my new friends, quiet quality time with Les was a must. Most of the time spent with the girls was when he was at a meeting, handling his workload, or if they came to one of the clubs he managed. One morning I woke up and watched him sleep. The sun rose and enveloped his black skin. His beard and goatee shimmered and the sun kissed his melanin. It reminded me of the poem I wrote the first time he left for Abu Khali.

When I See You Again
Preparing for the day we meet face to face again
Too long you have been gone
What's life without my best friend
The beauty that pours from your heart jump starts mine
Without you pulse reads low and life gets slower...come closer
When I see you I might just stop and stare
Because your presence is paralyzing...calm
I just might wrap myself around you
Intentions to never let go again
I've found beauty in our knowing who we are

49

What we are purposed to do and be in this life and
For each other.

My time away from Les allowed me to see that what we have is special. The finding of your soulmate is rare. But what's even more rare are people who actually escape, release, and heal from toxic relationships, traumatic memories, and self-induced mental imprisonment. Don't get it twisted, I have been through my own journey. I've won and I've lost. I fell and I got back up hundreds of times. But what I realized in the journey was the fact that I WAS NOT ALONE. When I realized that I could no longer wallow in a self-pity party because...GOD was there. I couldn't keep blaming other people for my personal choices and I, as a woman, had to take responsibility for myself.

I had to clean out the old so that my new could come. I had to look myself in the mirror and challenge myself to live my best life and walk in the power that was in me. When I acknowledged that I had the power of the God of the universe living in me something shifted in my thinking. I believed I deserved the best, fear left, and I believed I could accomplish anything I set my mind to.

I shared my story with the girls and I believe it triggered them to want the same. I do have a disclaimer... I am nowhere near perfect. Les and I continue to work toward perfection, but we offer a ray of hope because of our outward testimony of what love and God can do.

Well guys, I gotta go. I have a few more days left in Abu Khali before I go back to the states so the rest of my time will be spent with Les. As a matter of fact he's calling me now...A bientot!

COACHING CORNER

1.WHAT TOXIC THINGS, PEOPLE, THOUGHTS, OR HABITS ARE IN YOUR LIFE?

_____
_____
_____
_____
_____
_____
_____
_____
_____
_____
_____
_____
_____

2.WHAT IMPACT HAVE THOSE TOXIC AGENTS HAD ON YOUR LIFE & YOUR MENTAL AND EMOTIONAL HEALTH?

_____
_____
_____
_____
_____
_____

_____
_____
_____
_____
_____
_____
_____

3.ARE YOU READY TO FREE YOURSELF FROM TOXICITY?

_____
_____
_____
_____
_____
_____
_____
_____
_____
_____
_____
_____

4. IF YOU HAVE LISTED THE TOXICITY IN YOUR LIFE, THE IMPACT OF THAT TOXICITY, AND IF YOU'VE ANSWERED YES TO FREEING YOURSELF FROM TOXICITY THEN THIS IS WHERE THE TRUE WORK BEGINS.

A. WHO DO YOU NEED TO FORGIVE? WHAT DID THEY DO?

_____

_____

_____

_____

_____

_____

_____

_____

_____

_____

_____

_____

_____

B. FORGIVE THEM. THINK IT, WRITE IT, SAY IT.

_____

_____

_____

_____

_____

_____

_____

_____

_____

_____

_____

_____

_____

IF YOU ARE CRYING AT THIS POINT THEN ALLOW THE TEARS TO FLOW. IT IS A PART OF YOUR RELEASING! YOU ARE LETTING GO OF YEARS OF HURT, PAIN, TRAUMA, ANGER, BLAME AND UNFORGIVENESS. YOUR SOUL IS FINALLY BEING FREED TO LIVE ABUNDANTLY AND YOUR MIND NOW HAS ROOM TO RECEIVE.

C. DON'T GO THROUGH THIS TRANSITION ALONE. ALLOW PEOPLE THAT YOU TRUST TO COME IN AND WALK THIS JOURNEY WITH YOU. MAKE YOUR LIST OF PEOPLE IN YOUR TRIBE/INNER CIRCLE. AFTER YOU'VE MADE YOUR LIST INVITE THEM INTO YOUR JOURNEY.

_____

_____

_____

_____

_____

_____

_____

D. WRITE THE VISION FOR THE NEW YOU. WHAT DO YOU WANT? HOW ARE YOU GOING TO GET IT?

_____

_____

_____

_____

_____

_____

_____

_____

E. CHOOSE AN ACCOUNTABILITY PARTNER. THIS IS SOMEONE WHO WILL HELP YOU STAY IN LINE WITH YOUR VISION FOR THE NEW YOU. THROUGH THIS PROCESS YOU MUST REMAIN TRANSPARENT AND TRUTHFUL. LIST YOUR ACCOUNTABILITY PARTNER(S).

_____

_____

_____

_____

_____

_____

_____

I guess at this point you're wondering what you can and will accomplish if you try the steps listed above. I can assure you this, GOD WILL EXCHANGE YOU BEAUTY FOR YOUR ASHES (TOXINS).

We are fearfully and wonderfully made. We are also created to live an abundant life. Anything or anyone who does not honor you can't stay! You are a wonderful creation.

Yes, wonderful as in marvelous, glorious, sublime, lovely, first class, astonishing, stunning, awesome... Do you get my point? Which means that anything or anyone who doesn't acknowledge you for being all that you are...can't stay. YOU ARE ALL THAT!!!!!

Treese, Ngoyo, Nafisa, Jazmina, and Tao are all going through the journey now which is why I couldn't continue their stories. But what they did was start the process by acknowledging and sharing. We vowed to hold each other accountable to make sure we each live out our desire to be FREE! To be continued...

ABOUT THE AUTHOR

Ontaria Kim Wilson is a Philadelphia, Pennsylvania native. She lives her life dedicated to creating and sharing her art with the hope that lives will be touched and healing may occur where there is a need. She is a certified life coach, an accomplished dancer, and choreographer who has shared the stage with the legendary Teddy Pendergrass, Eve, Gina Thompson, and a host of live performing artists. She is an actress, writer and theater arts professional with over 25 years in the entertainment business. She appeared as an actress, writer, or director in over 17 film, stage, and television productions. A few notables are TV One's for My Man, Last Air Bender, Soul Train, Showtime at The Apollo, and From Teddy With Love (Teddy Pendergrass' last live recorded performance), Japanese Azteroids starring Darrin Henson and Jackie Christie, and more. She has over 50 dancing placements in celebrity performances. She has written and co-written featured films and animations. She is a co-author in Pen Legacy's Bruised, Broken and Blessed. Mostly recently she directed her first film "Call to Syria".Due to her extensive background she has taught and coached children and adults throughout the Delaware Valley (Pennsylvania, New Jersey, and Delaware) in the area of performing arts and motivational life skills in elementary schools, spiritual institutions, community centers, and performing arts schools. Her mantra is based on pouring into others so that the arts continue to thrive. She has served in leadership capacities in youth, dance, and missions ministries across the Tri State area as well.

Ontaria believes that following your passion, becoming aware of self, and walking in your truth is the source of her success.

THANK YOU

The person I am and the things I do would not be possible without God ordained people in my life. First and foremost, I have to pay homage **to my ancestors** for paving the way for me, for praying that their bloodline would prosper in spite of opposition. I thank you. To my grandmothers **Sylvia Wilson and Hattie Wilder** thank you for teaching me how to be a queen, how to stand tall in a crazy world, how to be an entrepreneur, how to not take crap from anyone. I love you both and miss you dearly...continue to rest well in glory. To my father **Paul Wilder,** Dad thank you for protecting me and teaching me the importance of being consistent and studious. Thank you for always challenging me to be the better me and to never let my integrity be questioned. Thank you for teaching me to cross every T and dot every I. And thank you for choosing me to walk with you during your fight with Leukemia. It grew me up and it taught me to stand firm in decision making when tough decisions had to be made. Thank you for choosing me to be the one who held your hand when you transitioned into glory. I love you and miss you beyond measure. Love "Stink".

To my queen, my rock, the vessel God used to bring me into this world, my mom, **Roslyn Wilson.** It would take the writing of another book to acknowledge you for everything you've been for me. But I'll squeeze as much in as I can. Thank you for teaching me what it means to be a woman and the importance of being consistent. Thank you for your life long sacrifice and love that you give me on a daily basis. Thanks for the tough love that pushed me to become the woman I am today. Thank for always having my back. I love you more than life itself. To my brother **Paul Wilson** and sister **Paula Wilder** you guys don't know this but I've always kept you in mind every time I had to make a life decision because I wanted to be the best example of what a big sister was supposed to be. Thank you for being my two little knuckleheads. Paul, thank you for always pushing me to be greater. Paula, thank you for always looking to me for advice...you always keep me on my toes. To my niece **Antavia Wilson** thank you for being you. Your encouraging words and love keep me going. Watching you grow has challenged me to be even greater. Keep dancing and being the authentic you. I love you my mini me. To all of my family thank you for your continued love and support throughout my life. I love you all to life.

To the love of my life, **Frank Lester**. Man, thank you for being you. Thank you for seeing greater in me than I see in myself at times. Thank you for your unwavering support and creative genius. Thank you for your patience, sacrifice, and understanding in all that I go through as an artist and as a woman. You are what my dad told me to expect when a man truly loves you.

To my tribe, my inner circle, my crew, my girlfriends thank y'all for being there through everything. Love you...especially you BFFs @ **Anisa Nyell Johnson** and my sister/friend **Danielle Shaw Ogelsby.** You ladies inspire me daily. Your strength and beauty are amazing.

To The Cast of Beautiful Toxicity 2018. You guys made this story come to life and inspired this book because people wanted more! Thank you!!!!!!!!

Charron Monaye! Thank you for being my sister, my friend, my coach, my accountability partner, and my publisher. You continue to challenge me and encourage me to be the BEST! Thank you for challenging me to GET OUT OF MY OWN WAY!

Last but absolutely not least I thank **God** for knowing me before I knew myself, for loving me and choosing me and giving me the power to be a change agent in this world.

Share This Book! Order More Copies

Retail Price $16.99

5-20 Books	$13.95 each
21-99 Books	$12.95 each
100-499 Books	$9.95 each

Special Quantity Discounts
To Place An Order Contact: ceo.ontariawilson@gmail.com